MY BIG BOY POTTY

by JOANNA COLE
illustrated by MAXIE CHAMBLISS

HarperCollins*Publishers*

Watercolors were used for the full-color illustrations.
The text type is 18-point Cooper Light.

Manufactured in China by South China Co. Ltd.

www.harperchildrens.com

Library of Congress Cataloging-in-Publication Data
Cole, Joanna.
My big boy potty / Joanna Cole; illustrated by Maxie Chambliss.
p. cm.
Summary: With the help of understanding parents, a young boy learns how to use his potty so he does not have to wear diapers any longer.
ISBN 0-688-17042-0
[1. Toilet training—Fiction.] I. Chambliss, Maxie, ill. II. Title. PZ7.C67346 Mx 2000
[E]—dc21 99-50286

16 17 18 19 20

❖

Michael is a boy just your age.

Michael likes playing with toys
and looking at books.
Do you like those things, too?

Michael wears diapers.
Do you wear diapers, too?

When Michael's diaper is wet or dirty,
he tells his mommy or daddy.
Then they put a new diaper on,
and Michael is clean and dry again.

One day, Mommy and Daddy
brought home a big box.
Do you know what was inside?
It was a new potty for Michael.

Michael tried sitting on the potty
with his clothes on.
Michael's bear Buddy sat
on the potty, too.
It was fun!

Daddy took off Michael's diaper.
He said, "Let's have potty time.
When you need to make pee-pee
or poop, please sit on the potty."

After a while, Michael's daddy said,
"Try sitting on the potty.
Maybe some pee-pee will come out."
Michael sat and sat.
But nothing went into the potty.

Later, Michael read his books.
"Try sitting on the potty," said Mommy.
"Maybe some poop will come out."
Michael sat and sat.
But nothing went into the potty.

Michael played with his toys.
Daddy said, “Try the potty again.”
Michael sat and sat.
This time something happened!

Mommy and Daddy and Michael
looked in the potty. They saw pee and poop.
"Michael used his potty!" said Mommy.
She hugged and kissed him.

Mommy helped Michael wipe himself.
Daddy helped him pour the
pee and poop into the big toilet.
Michael flushed the toilet.
The pee and poop went into
pipes under the house.
Then Michael washed his hands.
"What a big boy you are!" said Daddy.

At bedtime, Mommy put a diaper on Michael. "You'll still need a diaper at night for a while," said Mommy.

In the morning, it was potty time again.
Mommy took off the diaper,
and Michael used his potty.
Daddy showed Michael how to
stand up when he made pee-pee.

Every day Michael had potty time.
One day Mommy said, “Now you are very good at using your potty.
It’s time for big-boy pants.”
Mommy and Michael went to the store.
They picked out special big-boy underpants.

At home, Michael put the pants on. When he used the potty, he pulled the pants down. Michael liked to keep his new pants clean and dry.

One day Michael forgot to use his potty.
His pants got wet. The floor got wet, too.

"Don't worry," said Mommy. "All children have accidents sometimes."
Mommy helped Michael clean up.
She gave him clean pants.
"Next time you'll remember," she said.
And do you know what?
Next time Michael did!

You can be like Michael.
You can learn to use the potty, too.

Then won't you be proud of yourself!

Tips for Successful Potty Teaching

- Don't rush! Most children are not completely trained until around twenty-eight months. Some are earlier, some later.
- Get ready by telling your child that urine and feces come from his body. Help him learn to make the connection between the feelings of elimination and what comes out of his body.
- Wait for one or more of the following signs of physical and emotional maturity: Your child's diaper stays dry for a few hours at a time; he tells you when he is about to urinate or have a bowel movement; he asks to use the potty.
- Start by having a few hours of "potty time" every day or so. Remove the diaper and request that your child use the potty.
- Give friendly reminders to encourage success.
- Praise your child for *trying*, as well as for succeeding. Never scold or punish.
- Expect accidents! They are the best way for your child to learn that without a diaper he must use the potty.
- When your child is using the potty consistently, switch to underpants.
- Use a diaper at nap time and bedtime until your child is dry.
- Make your expectations clear: You are confident that your child will learn.